HEAVY LIFTING

ART AND STORY BY
SIGMAX

ADULT READERS ONLY

This is a work of ficiton.
All characters, events, and locations portrayed within are fictitious.

HEAVY LIFTING

Published by Bewere Books
Flagstaff, Arizona
https://www.bewere.net

ISBN 978-1-62475-158-5

Printed in the United States
First printing February 2022

Cover and interior art by SigmaX

SO DID HE.

COURTEOUS, RELIABLE, NEVER DIPPED ON A SHIFT.

PUT US TOGETHER, THOUGH...

2

3

SIG.

KIP.

GET AN EYEFUL OF THE NEW GUY YET?

YOU MEAN JOHNNY BRAVO?

NO, TOBY!

...

HMMM.

TOBY the DOBIE

-1 for rhyming

Wearing sunglasses indoors

Shirt too small on purpose

The gun show...impressive

Unknown quantity, further investigation required

ANY BETS ON WHO CRACKS THAT NUT FIRST?

MY MONEY'S ON YOU.

I DIDN'T THINK TOO MUCH OF HIM THEN. WHEN YOU'RE SURROUNDED BY MUSCLES AND DICKS EVERY NIGHT, ONE MORE STUD IN THE ROOM DOESN'T MOVE THE NEEDLE THAT MUCH.

SO MAYBE I'M DESENSITIZED.

THE BOYS MADE A SPORT OF IT, THOUGH.

WELL?

IS HE LOOKING THIS WAY?

...

I HAVE NO IDEA.

HE NEVER TOOK THE BAIT.

UN	MON	TUES	WED	THUR	FRI	
	1 ~~OFF~~	2	3	4 thirsty thurs	5 PRIDE—	6

THINGS WENT ON LIKE THAT FOR AWHILE.

HE WAS JUST A BLIP ON MY RADAR...

~~OFF~~						
~~OFF~~	15 cover for	16 LUAU night	17		18	

...AS I WAS ON HIS, I SUPPOSE.

SEE YA TOMORROW, SIG.

MHMM.

VRRR-TCH-TCH-TCH!!

FUCK!

7

9

10

1 millisecond...

2 milliseconds...

3 milliseconds...

twitch

WHEW! THAT'S A BIG ONE!

WHAT?!

THE POTHOLE. PRACTICALLY BIG ENOUGH TO FALL INTO, EH?

UH-HUH...

ANYWAY...
(AHEM)
YOUR ADDRESS.

RIGHT.

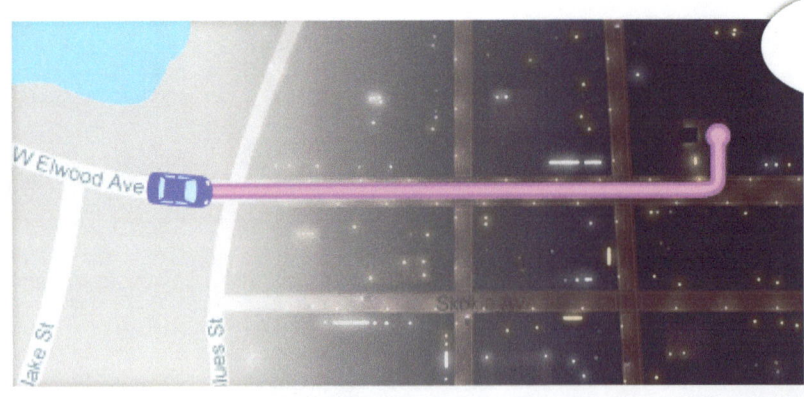

AAAND HERE WE ARE.

UHH...

OPEN 24hrs

...THIS IS A TRUFFLE HOUSE.

TRUFFLE HOUSE

76

YES IT IS. YOU HAVE A NICE NIGHT NOW!

HANG ON! THIS ISN'T THE RIGHT PLACE.

76 WEST ELWOOD, AS REQUESTED.

WEST?

YOU TWO HAVE A NICE NIGHT NOW!

WAIT, WE STILL HAVE ANOTHER STOP. YOU DIDN'T EDIT THE DESTINATION, DID YOU?

ARE THERE MULTIPLE ELWOODS?

I'M AFRAID I MUST INSIST YOU HAVE A NICE NIGHT OUTSIDE OF THE CAR NOW.

SO... DO THE DRIVERS USUALLY THREATEN YOU LIKE THAT?

NO, THAT WAS A FIRST.

SORRY.

IT'S FINE, I'LL JUST... CALL ANOTHER ONE.

OPEN 24hrs

LOOKS LIKE NEXT CLOSEST MINUTES AW

SO WE HAVE ABOUT 15 MINUTES.

76   TRUFFLE HOUSE

YOU WANNA WAIT INSIDE? I CAN ORDER SOME APOLOGY FOOD.

I TOLD YOU, IT'S FI-

GURGLE

ACTUALLY...

FOOD ACCEPTED.

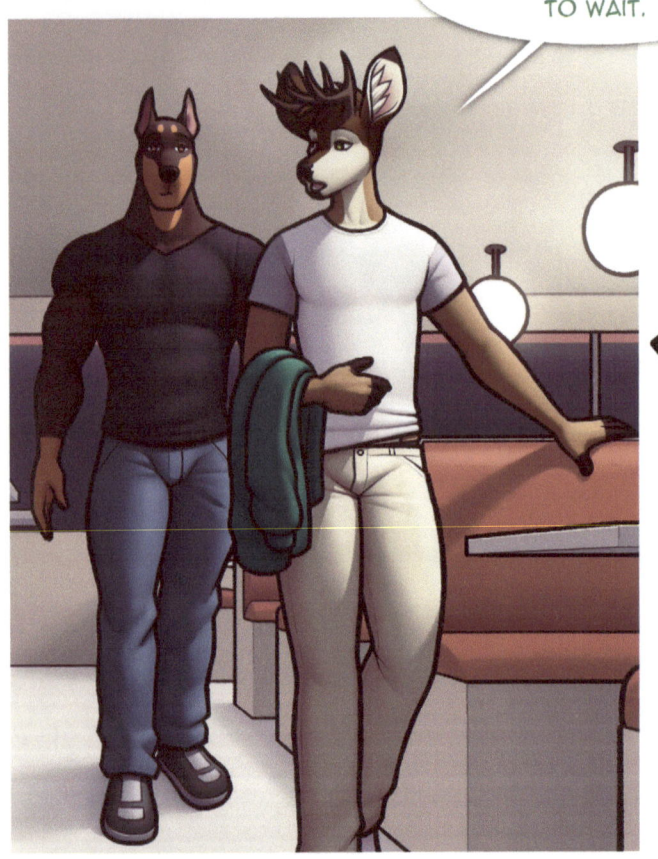

14

I STILL SAY THEY LOOK GOOFY.

I BET YOU'RE SCOPING OUT EYE CANDY THE WHOLE TIME.

CAN YOU BLAME ME? THERE'S A LOT OF IT.

SPEAKING OF WHICH...

IF YOU KNOW A FEW DANCE MOVES, YOU COULD PROBABLY MAKE SERIOUS BANK ONSTAGE YOURSELF.

IF YOU CARED TO SHOW OFF A BIT.

HAHA. I DUNNO IF I'M CUT OUT FOR THAT.

WHY NOT? DICK TOO SMALL?

WELL, YOU WOULD KNOW...

YOU PUT YOUR HAND *RIGHT ON IT.*

15

16

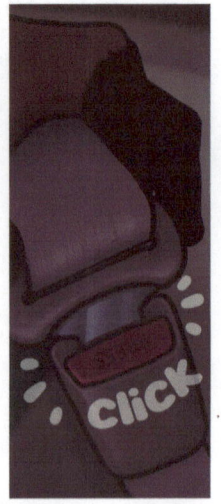

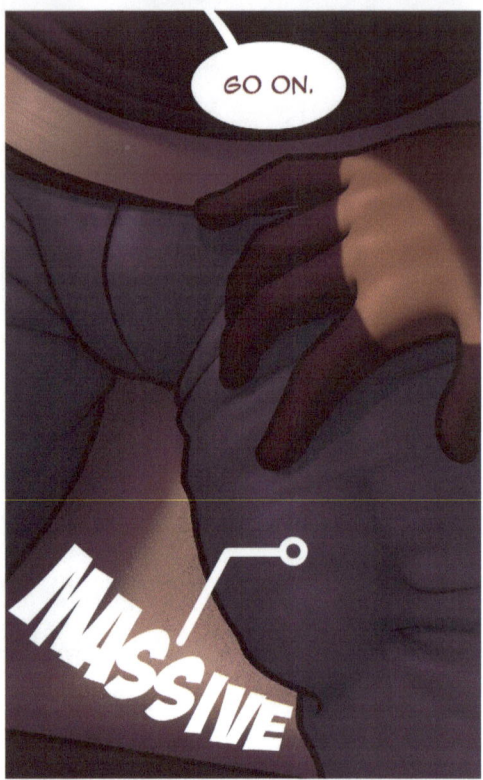

18

A BIT LATER...

...

AHEM.

OOF! *shuffle*

SORRY! *shuffle*

YOUR PLACE, HUH?
I WAS HALF-EXPECTING
ANOTHER TRUFFLE HOUSE.

HA!
NO SUCH LUCK.

PITY.

SO, UH...

...I GUESS THIS
IS KINDA LIKE
GOODNIGHT?
OR...?

OH.

YEAH,
KINDA.

...

ANYONE GETTING
OFF HERE?

cough

YEAH, THAT'S ME.
SORRY.

SEE YA AT WORK
TOMORROW, DEER.

19

HONEY...

WHAT?

YOU HAVEN'T BEEN HOLDING HIS DICK THIS WHOLE TIME JUST TO SAY GOODNIGHT.

click

VRRRRRMMM

DO YOU MIND IF I...?

uuah!

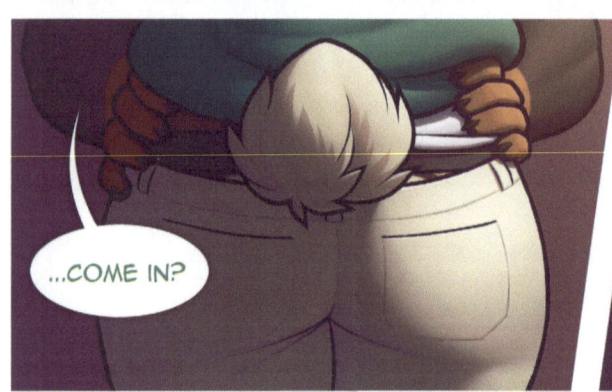

...COME IN?

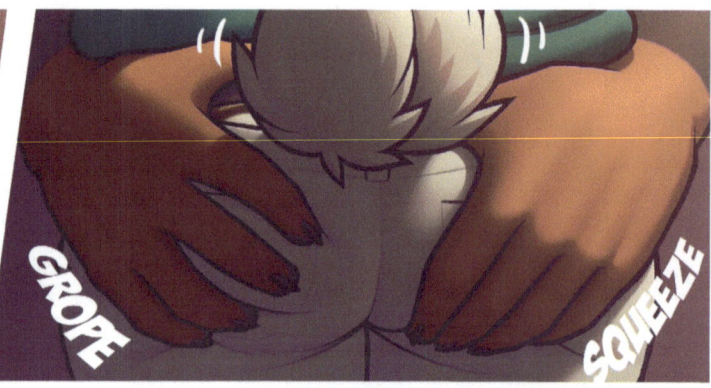

GROPE

SQUEEZE

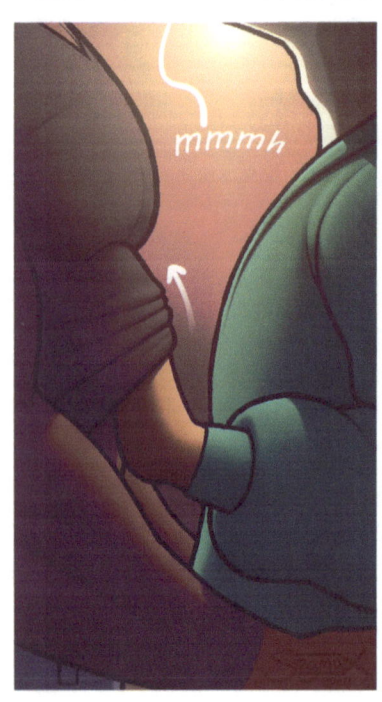

mmmh

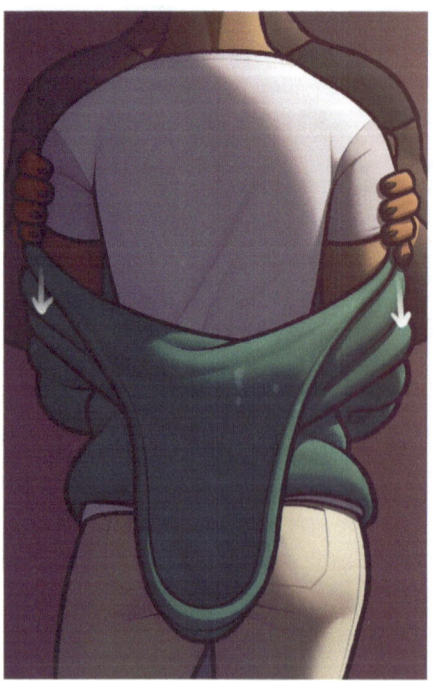

OOF!

shuffle

shuffle

SORRY-

HANG ON.

I'LL GET THE, UH...

...LIGHTS?

...

HEH. C'MERE.

SORRY. THIS HAPPENS.

I'LL BET IT DOES. PESKY ANTLERS.

YEAH...

23

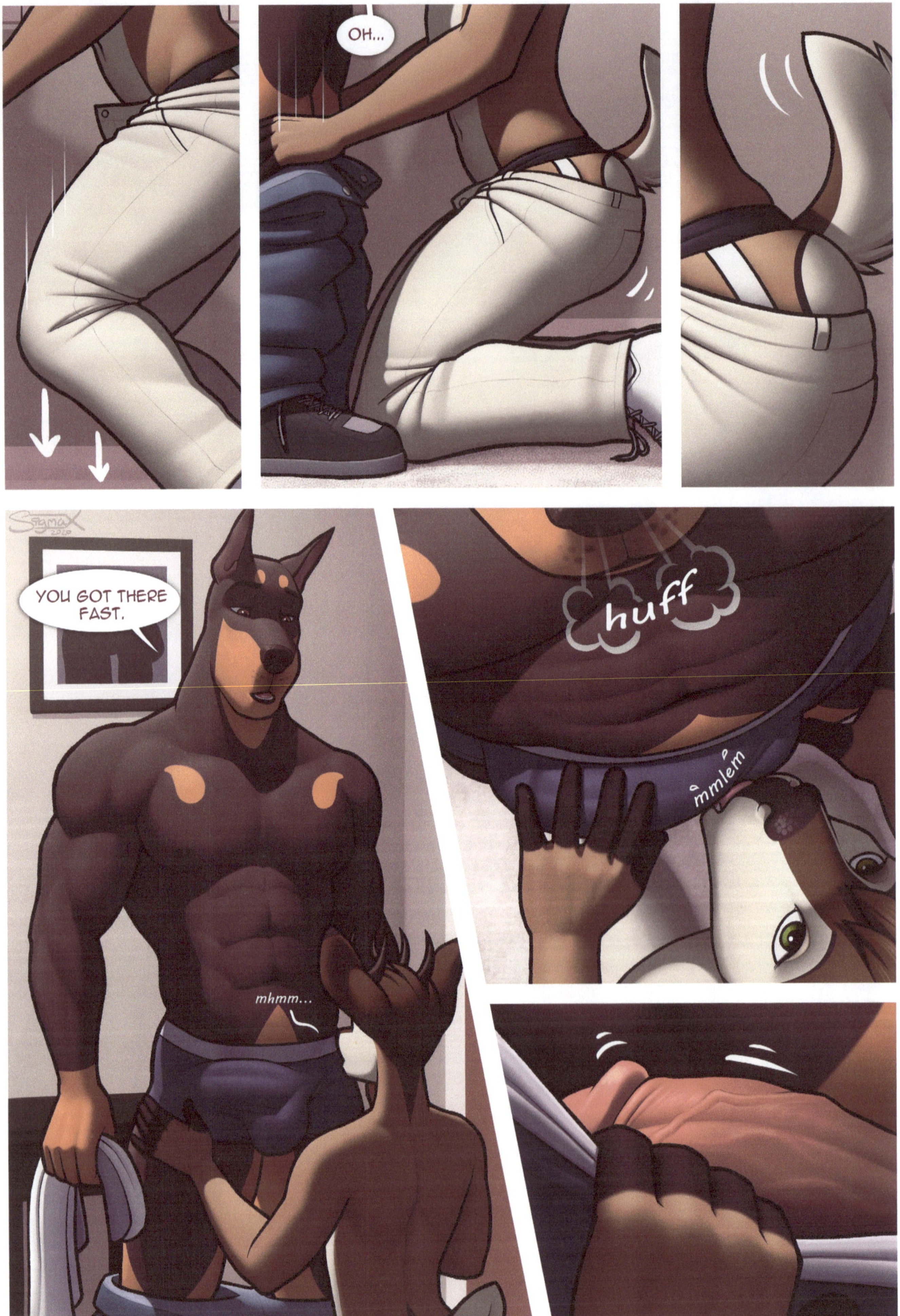

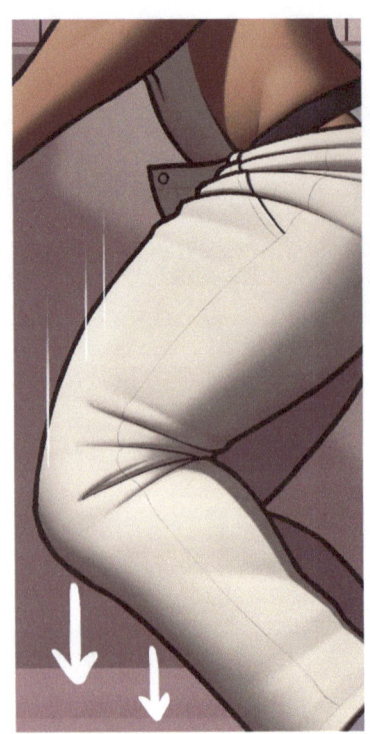

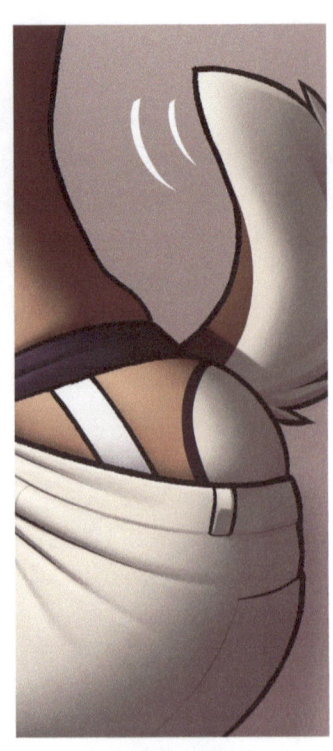

25

26

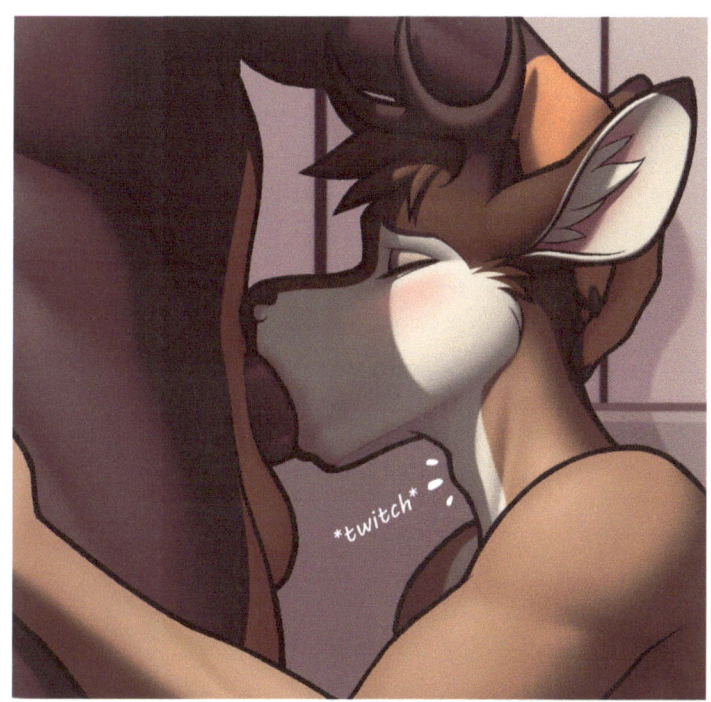

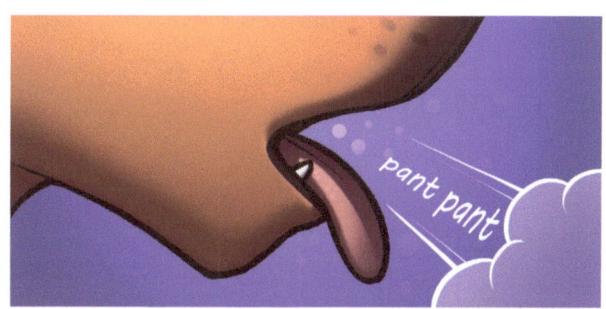

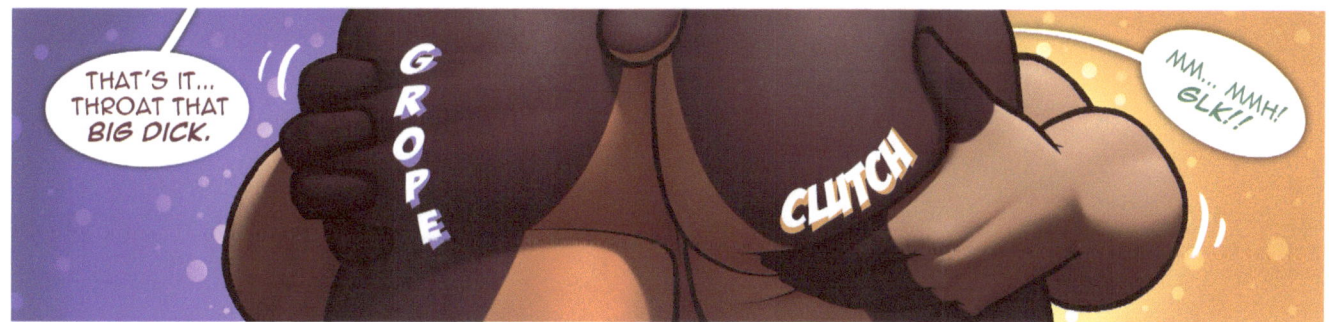

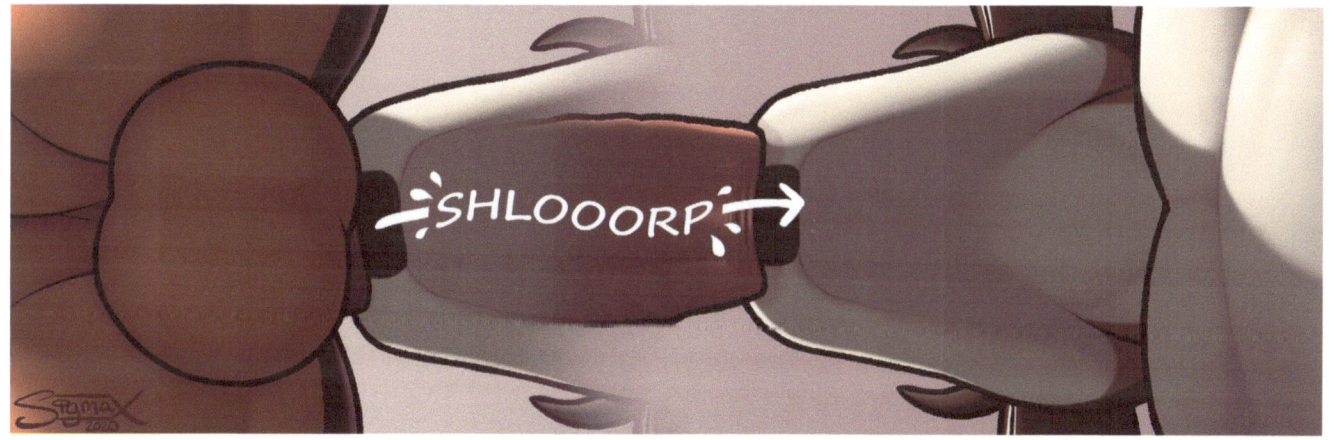

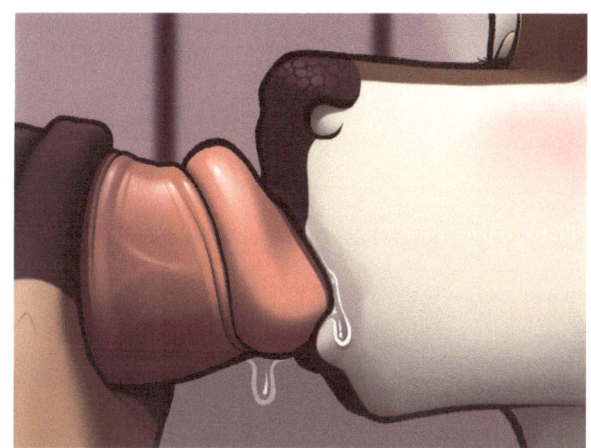

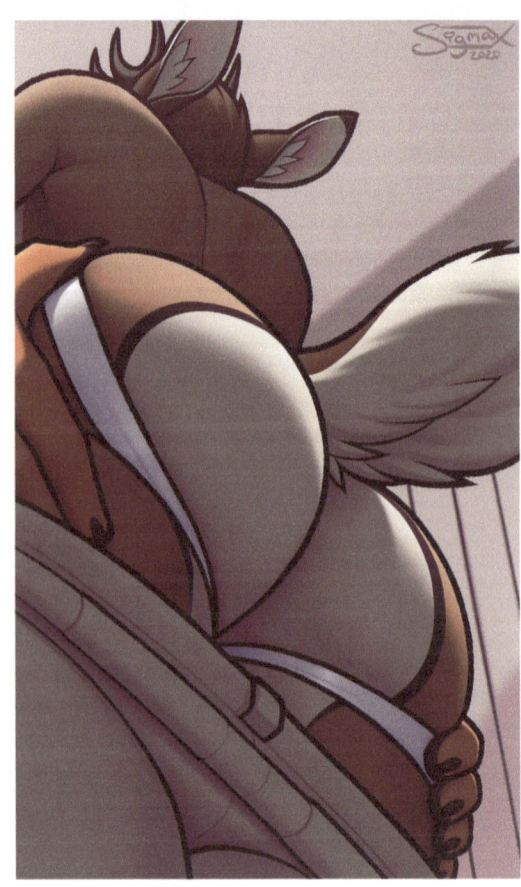

29

30

OOF! THIS IS COMFY.

I THINK WE CAN DO BETTER...

ARE YOU-?

RETURNING THE FAVOR.

OOH, TOBY...

kiss
kiss
kiss
kiss

Lick

JESUS.

31

33

SO, QUESTION FOR YA...

...DO DEER LIKE HOT DOGS?

TSCH! REALLY, TOBY?

HEH!

OKAY, YEAH I LIKE HOT DOGS.

BIG

HOT

SEXY DOGS.

this guy

34

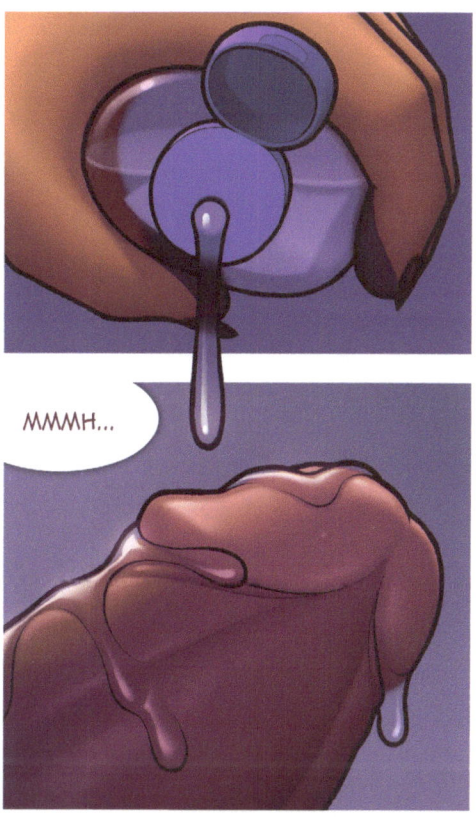

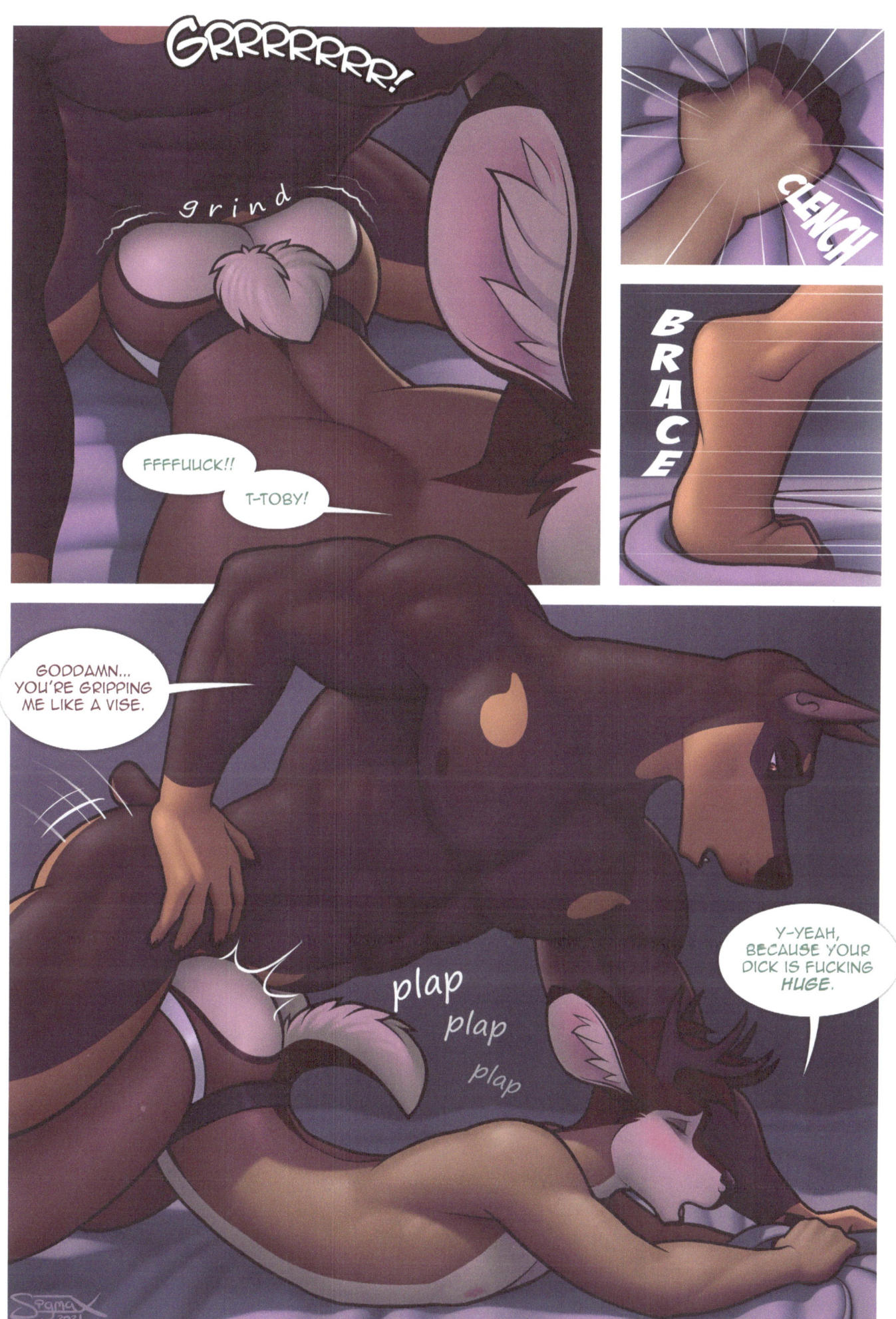

37

WELL, YOU DID KIND OF ASK FOR IT.

MMHMM... FEELS... SO GUHH...

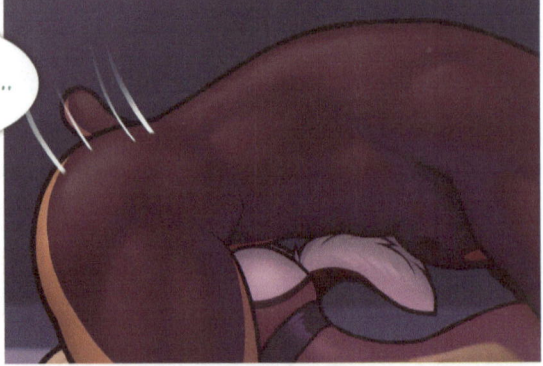

ΔΔHHN... YESSS...

JESUS... I'M KINDA CLOSE ALREADY.

FIRST LOAD ISN'T GONNA TAKE LONG.

HHNNG... GIVE IT TO ME, TOBY.

FUCKIN' GIVE IT TO ME!!

39

WE WASHED UP A BIT FIRST, OF COURSE.

...AND HE PUT ANOTHER LOAD IN ME.

I SLEPT SO FUCKING WELL THAT NIGHT.

WE DIDN'T WAKE UP UNTIL AFTER NOON...

...AND DIDN'T GET OUT OF BED UNTIL EVEN LATER.

Ah Ah Ah

glk glk

GOD, I COULDN'T GET ENOUGH OF HIM.

THERE WAS *SOMEONE* WHO HAD HAD ENOUGH, THOUGH...

MMF W-WAIT...

IS THAT...?

MY PHONE!

SHLORP!

HANG ON—

OOF!

—I'LL BE RIGHT BACK.

FUCK, MY EVERYTHING IS SORE.

Incoming C

Kip

HOOOH BOY.

RRFF!

AH AHH FUHH MMH GRRR

ARE YOU HAVING S E X RIGHT NOW?

WHA-?

N-NO

I'M JUST-

Sig

OKAY YEAH, KINDA. FUCK.

OH. MY. GOD.

I WANT THAT DICK OUT OF YOUR ASS THIS INSTANT! DO YOU HEAR ME, YOU WOODLAND COAT RACK?!

DON'T WORRY, I'M ALMOST DONE.

WAIT. IS THAT T-

Kip

boop!

45

THE END.